The Case of
the Giggling
Geeks

Tommy Nelson® Books by Bill Myers

Series

The Incredible Worlds of
Wally McDoogle

Picture Book
Baseball for Breakfast

www.Billmyers.com

SECRET AGENT
DINGLEDORF
...and his trusty dog, SPLAT

The Case of the Giggling Geeks

BILL MYERS

Illustrations
Meredith Johnson

NELSON

www.tommynelson.com

A Division of Thomas Nelson, Inc.
www.ThomasNelson.com

Text copyright © 2002 by Bill Myers
Illustrations by Meredith Johnson. Copyright © 2002 by Tommy Nelson®, a Division of Thomas Nelson, Inc.

Published in Nashville, Tennessee, by Tommy Nelson®, a Division of Thomas Nelson, Inc.

Library of Congress Cataloging-in-Publication Data

Myers, Bill, 1953–
    The case of the giggling geeks / by Bill Myers.
       p. cm — (Secret Agent Dingledorf . . . and his trusty dog, Splat ; 1)
    Summary: Ten-year-old Bernie Dingledorf is recruited as a secret agent to fight Dr. Chuckles, who is forcing the smart people of the world to laugh uncontrollably so that they will be what he wants them to be instead of what God wants them to be.
    ISBN: 1-4003-0094-0
    [1. Spies—Fiction. 2. Christian life—Fiction. 3. Humorous stories.] I. Title.
PZ7.M98234 Caq 2002
[Fic]—dc21   2002070934

Printed in the United States of America

06 RRD 11 10 9

This series is dedicated to
Laura Minchew—a fellow kid
no matter how much of a bigwig
she becomes.

*"Dear friends, let us love one another,
for love comes from God."*

—1 John 4:7 (NIV)

Contents

CHAPTER 1

The Case Begins . . .

Hey there. My name is Dingledorf. Bernie Dingledorf. At least, that's what my parents named me.

Unfortunately, I have another name, too.

But I'm already getting ahead of myself.

It all started at morning recess. I was trying to make my friend I.Q. play kickball. It was part of my plan to change him from a major geek into somebody majorly cool.

"Come on," I said. "Just step up to the plate and kick it!"

But I.Q. is not very good at sports. (Unless the sport involves turning on the computer, reading a billion books, or finding the cure for cancer.)

"Please don't make me." He sniffed and pushed up his glasses. I.Q. is always sniffing and pushing up his glasses. Probably because he has a ton of allergies and wears glasses the size of binoculars.

"If you don't go up there, you won't be cool," I said. "And if you're not cool, we can't be friends." It was kind of mean, but the only way I could get him to play.

He dropped his head, gave a sniff, and slowly walked to the plate. He was so scared he shook like a bowl of Jell-O on a jack-hammer in the middle of an earthquake.

They rolled the ball to him.

He leaned back and kicked with all of his might.

"ARGH . . . "

The kick was pretty good. It would have been better if he had actually hit the ball. Unfortunately, he missed it and

K-Thud

landed flat on his back.

"I.Q.!" I ran to him. "I.Q., are you okay?!"

Nothing seemed to be broken, except for his glasses.

After a moment he groaned and opened his eyes.

"I.Q., speak to me!"

It took all of his strength, but at last he moaned, "Can we still be friends?"

I just looked at him and quietly nodded.

By the time recess was over, I.Q. seemed pretty much okay. You'd never know he'd fallen except for the wad of tape we used to hold his glasses together. But that was all right. It was the third or fourth wad he'd used that week. (Like I said, he's not too good at sports.)

Now we sat in Mrs. Hooplesnort's fourth-grade class.

We were bruising our brains over multiplication tables. That's when things got a little weird.

First, there was the baseball that came

K-RASH-ing

through our window.

Of course, there was the usual leaping for cover and hiding under our desks.

And, of course, . . . all the girls screamed in fear (not to mention all the boys).

But where it got really weird was when Mrs. Hooplesnort didn't blow her stack.

She didn't go to the window and yell at the P.E. class outside.

She didn't even threaten to beat up the coach. (Don't laugh; being six feet, five inches tall, she could.)

Instead, she just looked down at the baseball as it rolled to a stop by her feet.

Then the weirdest thing of all happened.

She started to giggle.

Not a lot. At first it was just a little . . .

"tee-hee, tee-hee."

I glanced over at I.Q.

I.Q. glanced over at me.

Then it got a little bigger.

"Hee-hee. Hee-hee."

And a little bigger again.

"HO-HO, HO-HO."

"Mrs. Hooplesnort?" I asked. "Are you all right?"

She grabbed her sides. Then she began laughing so hard she could barely breathe.

"Mrs. Hooplesnort, what's wrong?"

"HAR! HAR! HAR!"

"Mrs. Hooplesnort?"

"HEE-HEE-HEE!"

I leaped from my desk and raced to her side. "Mrs. Hooplesnort! Mrs. Hooplesnort!"

She dropped to her knees.

"HO-HO!
HAR-HAR!
HEE-HEE!"

Tears streamed down her face as she laughed louder and louder . . . and louder some more.

"HEE-HEE!
HAR-HAR!
HO-HO!"

"Mrs. Hooplesnort!"

But, try as she might, the poor woman could not stop!

Now, you probably figure that's as weird as it gets, right?

Wrong.

After they loaded the giggling Mrs. Hooplesnort into the ambulance and after we all waved bye-bye, we headed to lunch.

And what's so weird about lunch, you ask?

(You obviously haven't eaten our cafeteria food.)

I grabbed a tray and stepped in line behind I.Q. "What are we having today?" I asked.

"It is difficult to tell for certain," he said. "It is either chopped liver and lima beans, or mashed potatoes and boiled Puppy Chow."

"Didn't we have that yesterday?" I asked.

"No." He sniffed. "That was either fried cauliflower or boiled kitty litter."

I watched as they dished up the goop and plopped it on our trays.

After loading up with the tasty tidbits, we headed for our table. Well, we tried to head for our table. But I.Q. was too busy tripping over his shoelaces, and accidentally dropping his tray

K-rash

onto the floor. (No biggie. He does that a couple of times a week.)

Of course, there was the usual clapping and cheering from the kids . . . and the usual red face from I.Q.

"I'm sorry, Bernie." He sniffed.

I reached down to help him up. "It's hard to be cool when you keep doing stuff like that."

"I'll try harder. Honest."

I nodded. "Just do what I do. Just think . . . *cooool*."

Before he could answer, one of the teachers from the teachers' table started to giggle. We turned to him.

His giggle turned to a chuckle. It grew until he was laughing out loud.

Everyone in the room stared at him, but he couldn't stop.

To make the weirdness even weirder, he picked up his own tray. Then he reached over and . . .

K-rash

dropped it onto the floor.

Unfortunately, it didn't just go *K-rash*, it also went

Ker-sploosh

as the liver and lima beans (or was it mashed potatoes and boiled Puppy Chow?) splattered up onto his red wool sweater.

But he didn't get angry. Instead, he laughed all the harder . . . which made the woman teacher beside him also start to laugh.

He saw her and reached down to his tray. He scooped up a handful of the goop and smeared it into her hair, which made them both laugh all the more.

What was going on?!

Then she reached into her tray and smeared the tasty goop all over his face,

. . . which made the teacher across from them start to laugh . . . until the first teacher wiped the gunk from his face and threw it smack-dab into the third teacher's face,

. . . which caused him to grab his food and throw it at another laughing teacher,

. . . which caused that teacher to throw it at another teacher,

. . . which—(Well, you probably get the picture.)

Soon, the entire teachers' table had broken out into a food fight. Chopped liver, lima beans, boiled Puppy Chow . . . you name it, it was flying.

And the more it flew, the more the teachers laughed. Louder and louder. Harder and harder.

Of course, none of us students were laughing. We just sat and stared.

What was happening? Why couldn't the teachers stop laughing?

A few minutes later we again stood in the parking lot waving bye-bye. This time it wasn't to Mrs. Hooplesnort. This time it was to a dozen different teachers being carted off in a dozen different ambulances.

But that didn't worry the teachers. They just kept on giggling and laughing.

Yes sir, things were definitely getting weird.

CHAPTER 2

The Plot Sickens

"Perhaps it is some sort of disease," I.Q. said. He sniffed and pushed up his glasses.

"Or maybe it's something in the water," I said.

"Or maybe *(sniff)* it's aliens attacking from outer space *(sniff, sniff)*."

"Better not be," said Priscilla, another good friend. "'Cause I'll send them running back to where they came from." To prove her point, she did a karate kick and spun around, chopping the air a bunch of times.

In case you haven't guessed, Priscilla has a black belt in karate, kung fu, and egg fu yung. Also, in case you haven't guessed, she hates the name *Priscilla*.

We turned the corner and headed up the street to our houses. Since there were no teachers left at school, there was no reason to stay—unless you wanted seconds on the cafeteria food.

But we'd already had enough food poisoning for the day, so we decided to head for home.

I turned back to I.Q. "Why does the laughing only happen to smart people, like teachers?" I asked.

"That's an excellent question," he said. "Perhaps—"

"Woof, Woof!"

I looked up just in time to see my trusty dog, Splat, waddling across the neighbor's yard to greet us. (He would have been running to greet us, but he'd had one too many Yummy Tummy Doggie Treats. Actually, he'd had one too many *boxes* of Yummy Tummy Doggie Treats.)

"No, Splat!" I shouted. "Use the sidewalk! Use the sidewalk!"

But he hates sidewalks. After all, Lassie and all the other cool TV dogs run across fields and jump over fences. Why couldn't he?

"Look out for the neighbor's wall!" I shouted. "Look out for the wall!"

But he raced toward it, planning to jump it with ease.

"Look out for the—"

K-SPLAT

(Well, at least now you know how he got his name.)

Before I could run over and scoop him off the ground . . . or give him mouth-to-mouth resuscitation (good thing those Yummy Tummy treats kill doggie breath), I heard

"tee-hee, tee-hee."

I turned to I.Q.
He was starting to giggle.

"Hee-hee. Hee-hee."

"What's so funny?" I asked.

"HO-HO."
(*sniff*)
"HO-HO."

"I.Q.?" Priscilla asked. "Are you okay?"

Soon, he was grabbing his sides, trying hard to catch his breath.

"HA! HA!"
(*sniff*)
"HAR! HAR!"

"I.Q.!" I shouted. "I.Q., can you hear me? I.Q., this is definitely uncool!"

But he was laughing so hard he couldn't answer. He dropped to his knees, laughing even louder.

"HO-HO!
HAR-HAR!
HEE-HEE!"

"I.Q.! I.Q.!"

Suddenly, there was another sound. But it didn't come from I.Q., and it didn't sound like laughter. Instead, it sounded like

whop-whop-whop-whop-whop.

Priscilla and I both looked up and shouted, "Helicopters!"

That's right. There were six helicopters coming down out of the sky.

"What's happening?!" I shouted.

"It's an alien invasion!" Priscilla yelled. "Just like I.Q. said!"

"But these are helicopters, not flying saucers."

"That's what they want us to think!" she cried.

The helicopters (or flying saucers) were landing all around us. A dozen soldiers (or aliens) leaped from them and ran straight toward us!

"What do we do?" I shouted.

"Don't worry!" Priscilla yelled. She crouched low and took a kung fu stance. "I'll hold them off!"

The men raced toward us. I'm not sure what they wanted, but by their angry faces I guessed they weren't selling Girl Scout Cookies. Oh yeah, and there was something else that said they meant business. . . .

They had guns!

Not guns like you see on TV. No way. These were pink and orange guns with cute little ribbons hanging from the barrels.

Cute little ribbons?!

(Did they really expect us to take them seriously with pink and orange guns . . . not to mention those ribbons?)

Before I could figure out what was going on, Priscilla went into action.

"Aiii-YAAAA . . ."

She leaped high into the air to deliver her first kick. But the leader dropped to his knee. He aimed his weapon and fired

zing-zing-zing-zing.

That's right. Not *K-Bamb*, not *K-Blewie*, not even the ever-popular *K-Pow,* but

zing-zing-zing-zing.

And instead of bullets, it fired little beams of light. Little beams of light that hit Priscilla in the face and froze her in midair!

It was just like those stop-action pictures in the movies. She was frozen in the middle of her jump.

"Wow!" I shouted. "You guys really are from outer space, aren't you?"

"Are you Ralph Dingledorf?" the Hot

Shot Leader asked.

"No, I'm *Bernie* Dingledorf," I said.

"Close enough," he said. He motioned to his men, and they grabbed me.

I figured it was time to be tough. It was time to fight back. It was time to scream and holler for my mommy.

But nothing I did helped. They just picked me up and carried me toward one of their helicopter/spaceship thingies.

"Don't worry, kid!" Hot Shot Leader shouted. "Nobody's going to hurt you!"

But, of course, I knew better. I'd seen enough *X-Files* reruns to know they were probably going to do experiments on my brain . . . or use it for football practice . . . or maybe both.

"Help me!" I shouted. "Help me!"

But nobody came to my rescue. Not

I.Q., who was still

"HAR-HAR,"
(*sniff*)
"HEE-HEE,"
(*sniff*)
"HO-HO"-ing!

And not Priscilla, who was still frozen in midair.

There was absolutely no one to help. No one except—

CHOMP!

"Yeow!" one of the soldiers yelled.

"What's wrong?!" Hot Shot Leader shouted.

"That stupid dog! He bit me!"

I looked over my shoulder and saw Splat. He'd finally woken up and had clamped down onto the rear of one of the men.

"Get him off!" the soldier shouted. "Get him off!"

"Later!" Hot Shot Leader ordered. "Right now, we have a job to do!"

The soldier jumped into the helicopter with Splat still hanging on.

I couldn't help smiling as they tossed me into the helicopter beside him. Good ol' Splat. I wasn't sure where we were going. I wasn't sure what they were going to do. But trusty Splat would stick with me to the end.

Not only my end, but by the looks of things, that soldier's end, too!

CHAPTER 3

Pick a Dingledorf,
Any Dingledorf

Eventually, we landed on some empty island with an elevator built into the side of a cliff.

Hot Shot Leader shoved Splat and me inside it. He waved bye-bye as the doors slammed shut. Suddenly, the two of us dropped faster than Mom's smile when she sees me tracking mud across the carpet.

Finally, the elevator slowed to a stop.

I looked at Splat.

Splat looked at me.

I whimpered.

Splat whimpered.

(We're not exactly the brave type.)

Then the elevator door slid open and . . .

"Wow!" I gasped.

In front of us was a huge hall with more TV screens than a Circuit City store. (And almost that many salesmen.)

But they weren't exactly salesmen. And they weren't exactly aliens. They were more like army guys.

"Ralph . . . ," one of them called to me.

I looked over to see this big guy walking toward me. Talk about muscles. He definitely worked out in the gym. And instead of weights, he probably lifted Volkswagens!

"Ralph Dingledorf!" He grinned. "So glad you could join us."

I frowned. "Uh, my name is Bernie," I said.

He frowned back. "What's that, Ralph?"

"Bernie."

"What do you mean, 'Bernie,' Ralph?"

"I mean, it's Bernie, not Ralph."

"Bernie who?"

"Bernie Dingledorf."

"You're confusing me, Ralph."

"Bernie."

"Bernie who?"

"Didn't we just go over that?"

Now, don't feel bad if you're getting con-fused. I know I was. Just as sure as my name was Ralph Dingle—er . . . Bernie Dingledorf, I knew there was a major mix-up.

I knew it. Unfortunately, Big Guy didn't.

"You are the famous secret agent, Ralph Dingledorf," he said.

"I am?"

"Yes. And since you are a master of

disguises, you've disguised yourself to look like a ten-year-old boy."

"I have?"

"Of course."

"Why?"

"Because you want to quit being a spy."

I frowned some more.

He continued some more. "But our agency discovered where you were hiding. And now we've brought you back here to our headquarters."

"You guys are pretty smart," I said.

"Thank you."

"Except for one tiny thing."

"What's that?"

"You're pretty wrong. My name is *Bernie* Dingledorf."

"Well, Ralph, whatever you call yourself, you are the only one who can save the world."

"From what?"

"The evil Dr. Chuckles."

"Who?"

He pressed a button on his wrist, and suddenly the floor under our feet disappeared. Not disappeared, really. It just sort of dropped out of sight. Causing us to sort of

"AAAUGHhhhhh . . ."

drop out of sight.

We landed softly on the next level. It had even more TV screens and people. But not all of the people were walking. Some of them were—

"EEEEeeee . . ."

"OOOOooo . . ."

"WAAAaaa . . ."

sailing high over our heads.

"What's going on?" I shouted to Big Guy. "Who are these people?"

"Secret agents, just like yourself."

We ducked as a man with flames shooting from his shoes

"YEOWwww . . ."

cartwheeled over our heads.

"What are they doing?!" I cried.

"Trying to use your cool gizmos. But as you can see—"

"LOOK OUT! COMING
THROUGH . . ."

We ducked as a human fireball flew over our heads.

"But as you can see," Big Guy repeated,

"none of them are as good at using secret agent gizmos as you. And without secret agent gizmos we won't be able to stop the evil Dr. Chuckles."

Another guy who was hanging on to a spinning umbrella

"Whoa . . . whoa . . . whoa . . ."

flew past.

"Who is this Dr. Chuckles?" I asked.

Big Guy snapped his fingers and another TV screen lowered in front of us. On it was a man with a red clown nose, a big painted smile, and a polka-dot bow tie that spun every time he laughed (which he did a lot).

"That's him?" I asked.

Big Guy nodded. "He's the one making all the brainy people laugh."

"You mean like Mrs. Hooplesnort?"

"Yes."

"And the other teachers?"

"Yup."

"And I.Q.?"

"That's right. He wants to turn all the supersmart people into superlaughers . . . just like himself."

"He can't do that," I said. "He can't make people laugh just because he wants them to."

"Why not? He laughs all the time."

"But that's him. He can't make everybody be like himself. They're people, too, you know. They're individuals!"

"I'm glad you feel that way."

"Why wouldn't I?"

"We've been watching what you've been doing with I.Q."

"What do you mean?"

Without a word he pressed another button. Suddenly, there was a videotape of I.Q. and me playing kickball.

"Come on," I was saying. *"Just step up to the plate and kick it!"*

"Please don't make me," he begged.

"If you don't go up there, you won't be cool," I said. *"And if you're not cool, we can't be friends."*

I turned to Big Guy. "What's that got to do with anything?" I asked.

"Just as Dr. Chuckles wants to change all the geeks into gigglers like himself . . . you want to change I.Q. into being cool like yourself."

"That's completely different," I said.

"Is it?" he asked. "Instead of letting God make I.Q. into who He wants him to be, you're trying to make I.Q. into who *you* want him to be."

"Yeah, but—"

Big Guy turned to me and waited for an argument. Unfortunately, *"Yeah, but,"* was the best I could do.

He reached over and pressed another button. A dozen more TV screens lit up. On every screen, somebody was laughing.

Like the lawyer who was . . .

"Hee-Hee-Hee . . ."

rolling around on the floor in front of a jury.

Or the next screen where a doctor was trying to give his patient a shot but kept . . .

"Ho-Ho . . ."
"Ouch!"
"Ha-Ha . . ."
"OUCH!"

missing.

And let's not forget the scientist who was busy mixing chemicals until he

"Har-Har-H—"
K-BLAAAM!!!!

accidentally blew up his lab.

Big Guy cleared his throat. "All of this is the work of the evil Dr. Chuckles."

"How are you going to stop him?" I asked.

"We're not," he said.

"You're not?"

"No."

"Then who?"

"You."

"You who?" I asked.

"You who," he said.

"Me who?"

He nodded. "Come, Secret Agent Dingledorf. We have much to do. . . ."

CHAPTER 4

And Away We GOooo . . .

Big Guy, Splat, and I stepped into the coolest room of all.

It had all sorts of electric gadgets, do-dads, and thingamabobs . . . with more flashing lights than a Christmas tree gone crazy.

"What is this place?" I asked.

"The Gizmo Lab," Big Guy said. "Surely, you remember. This is where we invent all your secret agent gizmos."

I pointed to one table where a bunch of scientists were working. "What are they doing?"

"They're working on a combination wrist watch and time machine."

"Wow!"

"Yes," he sighed. "But every time they press a button to check the time . . . they wind up being chased by dinosaurs!"

"Needs a little work?" I asked.

"Needs a lot of work," he said.

"And over there?" I pointed to some more scientist types.

"They're working on an automatic nose blower."

"An automatic nose blower?" I asked. "Why would anyone want an automatic nose blower?"

"That's what they're working on."

"And over there?" I pointed to another table.

"Singing toilet paper."

I gave him a look.

"Don't ask." He shook his head. "Don't even ask."

We continued walking through the room.

"These are the types of gizmos that you are famous for using," he said. "These are what you must stop Dr. Chuckles with before he *hee-hee . . .*"

"Pardon me?" I asked.

"I said these are the gizmos that *tee-hee, tee-hee . . .* you must *ho-ho-ho . . .* Oh, no!" Big Guy cried. "It's happening to *har-har-har* me, too!"

"You mean the giggling?!" I cried.

"Yes, *yuck-yuck-yuck!*" he shouted. "Quick!" He raced over to some shelves and returned with a giant backpack.

"In here are all the gizmos you'll need!" he yelled. "You know *hee-hee . . .* what to *ho-ho . . .* do with—*har-har-har-har . . .*"

But he could not finish the sentence.

"Mr. Big Guy!" I shouted. "Mr. Big Guy!"

But it was too late. He was already on the floor laughing.

And not just him.

I looked around the Gizmo Lab. All the scientists were doing the same thing. Each and every smart person was laughing his or her head off. Everyone but me (which probably says something about my smarts).

"What am I supposed to do?!" I shouted.

But nobody could answer.

"Somebody tell me what to do!"

Repeat in the Nobody-Could-Answer Department.

I bent down to the backpack and opened it.

There was nothing fancy inside. Just everyday stuff like tennis shoes, some shirts, a belt, a wristwatch with a trillion buttons on it, some dental floss, and on

and on and on . . .

I picked up the dental floss. *How could stuff like this stop Dr. Chuckles?* I wondered.

I pulled out some of the floss. *I mean, it's only—*

K-VROOOOM!!!

The tail end of the dental floss fired up just like it was a rocket. The reason was simple. . . .

It was a rocket! It was jet-powered dental floss!

Before I knew it, the thing

K-WOOOOSH!!!

took off.

I guess that wouldn't have been so

bad. Except for one small detail.

I FORGOT TO LET GO!

(Sorry, didn't mean to yell. But you try hanging on

to jet-powered dental floss without yelling.)

So there I was, flying around the room, hanging on for dear life . . . with Splat hanging on to *me* for dear life.

Around and around we flew.

And around some more.

Everywhere we went, we left a trail of dental floss. Not just around the room. But around those poor scientists, too.

That's right. They were getting tied up faster than Dad trying to hang our outdoor Christmas lights.

Things were definitely getting weirder in a bigger way!

CHAPTER 5

Will Someone Answer That Underwear?

It wasn't too long before my dental floss ran out of fuel (and floss).

Eventually, Hot Shot Leader showed up. He cut everyone loose and took me home.

Ah yes . . . home.

Home, where everybody listens to your troubles.

Home, where you can explain giant mix-ups like becoming a secret agent.

Home, where you have three older sisters and are lucky to squeeze a word in edgewise!

Now, I don't want to say that my sisters talk too much sometimes.

They talk too much all of the time!

Ever been in a room where the TV set is blaring and no one is really listening? That's like my house. Only it's not just one TV set blaring, it's three—two blonds and one redhead.

With no MUTE button!

I got home just in time for dinner and raced to the table. "Guys, guys!" I shouted. "You won't believe what happened to me!"

"You're interrupting," Sister 1 said in her usual snooty voice. "I hope you'll have more manners when Kevin comes over for dinner."

Sister 2 showed equal interest in me: "So Julie tells Jenny not to tell Janey what Jimmy told Jason about—"

"People think I'm a secret agent!" I cried.

Sister 3 answered by asking, "So do you think the pink sweater with my white blouse makes me look too fat?"

"Guys!" I cried.

"Please, stop shouting." Sister 1 rolled her eyes. "I don't want Kevin to think our family is totally nutzoid."

"But I've got secret agent gizmos and everything!"

I turned to my mother. "Mom, they want me to save the world!"

"That's nice, sweetheart. Now, eat your asparagus. Even secret agents need their vegetables."

I turned to Dad, but decided to save my breath. As a father of three teenage girls, he had learned the importance of "zoning out." It's the ability of his body to be in one place and his mind to be a thousand miles away (or at least in the next room watching ESPN).

Not that I blamed him. I mean, in our family, "zoning out" was the only way not to go deaf—

". . . Jordan telling Judy about Joshua not telling Junie . . ."

—or go crazy.

". . . how 'bout I wear my blue pullover with my tweed skirt?"

So, after carefully hiding my asparagus under a piece of bread, I headed upstairs to my room.

Somehow, I figured tomorrow was going to be a busy day. Unfortunately, my figurer couldn't have figured more right.

The next morning Priscilla and I walked to school. I.Q. stayed at home.

"So how long were you frozen in the air like that?" I asked.

"Just until you left with those guys in the spaceships," she said.

"They were helicopters."

"Yeah, right. Like I said, that's what they *want* you to think."

We entered our classroom and sat down.

"I still don't see why they think this Dr. Chuckles is so bad," Priscilla said.

"Because . . . he's forcing people to be how *he* wants them to be, instead of how God made them."

"Oh," she said. "Kinda like how you're forcing I.Q. to be cool?"

I winced. "Is that really what I'm doing?"

Suddenly, there was a loud . . .

beep-beep-beep-beep.

She turned to me. "You didn't tell me you had a cell phone," she said.

I frowned. "I don't." I looked down at my pants pocket. But it wasn't exactly coming from my pocket.

beep-beep-beep-beep

"Then what's ringing?" she asked.

"I think—" I lowered my head to hear better. "I think it's . . . my underwear."

"Your what??"

"My underwear. I'm wearing a bunch of secret agent clothes from the backpack they gave me. It's all pretty cool, but—"

beep-beep-beep-beep

"What do I do?" I asked.

She looked around nervously, then said, "Answer it."

I dropped my head and said, "Hello?"

Suddenly, a voice asked, "Secret Agent Dingledorf?"

"Uh, yeah, this is Dingledorf."

"You've got to join us!"

"Now?"

"Yes. We've found Dr. Chuckles's hideout. It's time for you to make your move."

"Where? How?"

"Just head for home. We'll pick you up."

CLICK

That was it. He hung up.

How odd.

But not as odd as looking up and seeing the entire classroom staring at me. And not just the class . . .

The substitute teacher was standing directly over me.

I looked at her and swallowed. "I, uh . . . I gotta go."

"Go?" she asked with concern.

"Yeah, I gotta go, bad."

She pointed to the door. "If you gotta go, you gotta go."

I leaped from my chair and raced for the door.

She obviously had a different version of "going" than my version of "going." But it didn't matter. At least my "going" helped me go until I was gone.

CHAPTER 6

"Dr. Chuckles, I Presume."

I raced home faster than Dad goes for the aspirin after seeing my sisters' phone bill.

I turned the corner to my street and saw . . . a giant hot-air balloon with a basket. It floated just inches above the ground.

A man stood inside the basket. He wore a clown suit, a big red clown nose, and a painted smile. Call me overly suspicious, but I was, er, uh, overly suspicious. Not only because of his clothes and makeup, but because of his constant . . .

tee-hee, tee-hee-ing.

"Who are you?" I asked.

But there was something about his clothes, his face, and his laughter that told me I already knew. Then, of course, there was the giant sign on the balloon that read:

DR. CHUCKLES

I put all these clues together and came to a brilliant answer.

"Dr. Chuckles?!" I gasped. (I told you it was brilliant.)

He let loose another giggle. Then, in his kindest voice, he screamed:

"GET HIM!"

Suddenly, three men, slightly bigger than gorillas, appeared. They jumped from the basket and grabbed me. Well, at least, they tried to. . . .

But the first guy had barely touched my new secret agent shirt before electricity . . .

K-ZAP!

shot into his hands. (Talk about a shocking experience.)

I don't want to say it was a lot of electricity, but I did notice Gorilla Guy sort of glowed like an x-ray before passing out on the ground.

The next gorilla tried to grab me around the waist.

But as soon as he touched my secret agent belt, a dozen Ping-Pong paddles popped out. They started spinning around the belt and . . .

k-thwap, k-thwap,
k-thwap-ing

his hands, his arms, and anything else
that got in their way, including his . . .

K-Thunk

head, which caused him to also

"Augh . . ."
K-Thud

join his partner in unconscious land.

Two gorillas down, one to go.

Unfortunately, it was about this time
that my trusty dog, Splat, . . .

"Woof! Woof!"

waddled to my rescue.

Once again he tried to race across the neighbor's yard.

"No, Splat!" I shouted. "Stay, boy! Stay!"

But his master was in danger. Splat had to be a hero. He had to leap into the air at the bad guys and—

K-Splat.

If you guessed that's the sound dogs make when they hit hot-air balloon baskets, you guessed right.

"Splat!" I yelled.

I raced to him and scooped him into my

arms . . . just as Gorilla Guy #3 scooped both of us into *his* arms.

It was a thoughtful act. I appreciated his kindness. I would have appreciated it more if he hadn't . . .

"Augh!" *k-plop*
"Augh!" *k-plop*

tossed us into the basket.

Even that wouldn't have been so bad if the balloon hadn't started to lift off.

Call me a worrywart, but somehow I suspected we were NOT on our way to visit Dorothy and To-To.

Dr. Chuckles's hideout was awesome. If the place was any cooler, they'd make you wear scarves and mittens. It's hard to explain, but just imagine . . .

—5 Chuck E. Cheese restaurants

—3 carnival fairgrounds

—and a bunch of Toys "R" Us stores

all dumped into a blender and turned on *high*.

Of course, the place was a mess. I don't want to say the guy was a slob, but picture my family bathroom on Friday night after all three sisters have used it to get ready for their dates.

"What do you think?" Dr. Chuckles giggled as we waded through two or three thousand beach balls lying all over the floor.

"Cool," I said. "For a bad guy's hideout, this is pretty good."

"I'm not really bad," he said as he reached up and . . .

his clown nose.

"I don't know," I said. "Trying to make all those smart people be like you, when they don't want to be . . . that sounds pretty bad to me."

"I'm just helping them have fun." He giggled.

I shook my head. "You're trying to make them into something *you* want them to be, instead of what God wants."

"Don't be such a spoilsport." He made his bow tie spin to try to get me to laugh.

I didn't.

He did it some more.

I didn't laugh some more.

"Okay, fine. If that's the way you want to be," he said. "Follow me. I'll show you something that will really make you laugh."

We climbed up two rope ladders and slid down three giant slides. Then we walked through a huge house of mirrors until we finally arrived at a gigantic machine.

It was the strangest thing yet. Just picture . . .

—100 empty toilet paper tubes glued end to end

—2 gigantic eggbeaters turning and attached to those tubes

—about 1,000 tricycle wheels (complete with turning pedals)

—and 3 giant Slinkys going back and forth and back and forth.

"What is it?" I shouted over the noise of the Slinkys.

"It's my **S**ure **M**akes **I**ntelligent **L**osers **E**ager to **S**mile machine."

"What?" I asked.

"I call it S.M.I.L.E.S. for short," he yelled. "I just point it at one of my satellites, like so."

He typed a bunch of numbers on a computer keyboard. The giant toilet paper tube moved.

"Then I type what group I want to hit. Let's see, how about . . ."

He typed out the word:

DRIVERS

"Now a beam will shoot out this tube, bounce off my satellites, and cause every driver in the world to begin laughing."

"You mean, like, drivers of cars?" I asked.

"Yes," he said. "And buses and trucks. Every driver in the world will laugh so hard that they'll all crash into each other

. . . which will make them laugh even harder."

"You're not serious?"

"I'm not?" he said. "Just watch!"

He reached over and pressed another button. It was labeled: STANDBY.

The eggbeaters beat harder.

The Slinkys slinkied faster.

Then he reached for the green button. The one labeled: START.

It was now or never. I had to act fast. I had to stop him.

If I didn't, our freeways would be more dangerous than . . . than . . . when my oldest sister got her driver's license!

CHAPTER 7

Ready, Aim, . . . Fling!

I leaped for Dr. Chuckles, but his gorilla boys suddenly appeared and grabbed me.

I had to do something. Then I remembered my gizmos. I looked at my new watch. The one with the trillion buttons on it.

Which one to press?

Using the scientific method of "Eenie-meenie-minie-moe," I closed my eyes, stuck out my finger, and pushed.

Suddenly,

ding . . . ding . . . ding . . .

there were three exact copies of myself. Well, four, if you count me.

"Cool, cool, cool, cool," I, er, we all said.

The only problem was when one of us did something, we all did it. So when I jumped at the doctor, all four of us jumped

K-smash

into each other.

Of course, Dr. Chuckles thought this was the funniest thing since Barney the dinosaur.

"So, you want to fight?" He giggled.

"No, no, no, no," we all said.

He turned and typed something else into the computer.

Suddenly, a gazillion and a half banana cream pies rose up from the floor all around us.

"All right, boys!" he shouted to his assistants. "Get 'em!"

The gorilla guys grabbed the pies and started . . .

fling, fling, fling-ing

them at us. Which meant we all got hit smack-dab in the

k-splish, k-splash

face.

Well, we all got hit but Splat. He was too busy running around

k-SLUURRRP-ing

up all of the pies he could find. (I did mention he likes to eat, right?)

Of course, the four of me grabbed more pies and started

fling, fling, fling-ing

them right back at the bad boys, which caused more

k-splish-ing and *k-splash*-ing

along with even more

k-SLUURRP-ing

not to mention a little

K-BURP-ing.
(I tell you, for a little dog, he can really put it away.)

The war continued. It was hard to tell who was winning.

Then I saw Dr. Chuckles reach over and type something else on the screen. Instead of $DRIVERS$ the screen now read:

$$EVERYONE!$$

"NO! NO! NO! NO!" we shouted. But it was too late.

He reached over and hit the $START$ button.

Suddenly, the machine . . .

hummmmmmm-ed

to life. A bright, green beam shot out of the long tube.

All four of us raced to stop him. But

the banana pie goop caused us to slip and
slide all over the

> "WHOA!"
> "WAAH!"
> "WEEE!"
> "WOOO!"

floor.

I got up and saw one of my secret agent shoes was untied. I gave the lace a tug and suddenly . . .

shhweesh-shhweesh-shhweesh

the shoelaces from both of my shoes began growing and shooting out.

But not just my shoelaces. The shoelaces of all four of me. Every lace was growing hundreds of feet long!

That's not all. As they grew, they wrapped around everything they touched: gorilla guys . . . chuckling bad boys . . . photocopied Dingledorfs.

In seconds we were all wrapped up—packed tighter than Uncle Elmer's shirt after Thanksgiving dinner.

But the laces didn't stop there.

They whipped up even higher until they started to

shhweesh-shhweesh-shhweesh

wrap around the tube of the S.M.I.L.E.S. machine.

They pulled the tube so tight that it tilted down.

Now it was pointed directly at . . . Dr. Chuckles!

Now the green beam was firing at him!

Now he began to laugh. But not the little *tee-hee*s or *hee-hee*s. No way. These were giant

"HARDY-HAR-HAR-HARS."

He turned to us. "Shut it off!" he begged. "Please—"

"HOO-HOO-HOO!"

" . . . shut it—"

"HEE-HEE-HEE!"

"off!" But the S.M.I.L.E.S. beam just kept firing. Soon it was bouncing off him and hitting everyone else in the room. Sooner still, everyone was laughing. . . .

Dr. Chuckles:

"HO-HO-HO!"

Gorilla guys:

"HAR-HAR-HAR!"

And yes, even me . . . actually, all four of me:

"YUCK-YUCK!"
"YUCK-YUCK!"
"YUCK-YUCK!"
"YUCK-YUCK!"

There was no way to stop it. The beam just kept on firing, and we just kept on laughing.

What could we do?
How would we ever stop laughing?
How would we ever save the world?
More important, would Splat ever stop

K-slurp slurp slurp-ing

up all those banana cream pies?

CHAPTER 8

The Case Closes

So there we were, tied up and laughing our heads off.

There was no way out. No way to get free. No one to save us. Except . . .

K-slurp-slurp
BURP!

"Splat!"

I looked up and called between my giggles, "Come *ho-ho-ho, hee-hee-hee* here, boy!"

But I couldn't get his attention. He was too busy playing doggie vacuum cleaner with the pies. By the looks of things, he wasn't going to quit until he got the whole place licked clean.

K-slurp-slurp
BELCH!!
(Wow, that was a good one.)

He was nearly done when he saw it. Up on the S.M.I.L.E.S. control panel. One last banana cream pie. It was close to the OFF switch.

He leaped for the panel. Unfortunately, his leaper was a little loaded (500 banana cream pies will do that). So he . . .

K-SPLAT-ed

back onto the floor, face-first.

But mighty Wonder-dud, er, dog would not give up. He knew what he had to do. He knew he was our only hope. (He also knew that was the very last banana cream pie.)

Again he tried and again he

K-SPLAT-ed.

But if there is one thing my dog knows, it's how to keep trying. (And to keep eating.)

He leaped one last time and . . . made it!

"HO-HO-Hooray!"

we all shouted.

In a moment, he started gobbling down the pie.

In less than a moment, one of his pudgy paws accidentally hit the OFF switch.

Instantly, the machine . . .

hummmmmmmm-ed

down until all its power was gone.

Once we untied ourselves, we all clapped and cheered and treated Splat like a hero. (He might have enjoyed being a hero, if he hadn't been so busy eating like a pig.)

I looked over at Dr. Chuckles. He sat on the floor, catching his breath.

"Are you all right?" I asked.

"It was awful. I couldn't stop laughing," he said as he dug banana filling out of his ear. "It was terrible."

"That's what I was saying. You shouldn't force people to be something they're not."

He nodded. "Like you said, 'God created each of us differently.'"

"Exactly. And we should respect and love people, even if they're different from us."

He repeated the words, *"Respect and love."* Slowly, he rose to his feet. "I think I get it now."

"Great."

"Listen, do you want to stay for dessert? I've got some extra banana cream pies in the freezer."

"Uh...no, thanks," I said. "I'm kinda sick of those."

"Oh," he said. "Well, I guess I can *respect* that decision." He broke into a grin. "And still *love* you. *'Respect and love,'*" he repeated. "I think I really am getting it!"

I grinned back. "I think you really are. . . . And I think I'm finally starting to get it, too."

After a bunch of good-byes and stuff, Splat and I finally headed for home.

We both knew the world would be a lot

more respectful and loving place to live. (Though maybe not nearly as funny.)

We also knew that our work was done. Our first and last job as secret agents was over.

Well, maybe our first job.

But not exactly our last.

Later that night, I.Q. swung by the house. Well, at least I thought it was I.Q. But when I opened the door, I saw some kid in baggy shorts and sunglasses, wearing about a hundred press-on tattoos.

"I.Q.?" I asked.

"'Sup, bro?"

Splat trotted to my side and gave a little growl.

"It's okay, boy," I said. Then I turned

to I.Q. and asked, "What are you doing in that getup?"

"You gave me, like, the 411 on getting down and getting cool 'fore we could hang, so I got me some happenin' threads."

"Oh," I said, holding back my laughter. "Listen, about that. I was wrong trying to make you into someone you aren't. I shouldn't have tried to make you—"

"And I bought this awesome kickball, too."

"Well, that's great," I said, "but I really shouldn't have tried to—"

"Figure you could give me some what-up pointers."

Before I could answer, he turned and started down the porch steps.

"Listen, I.Q., I was wrong about all that. You don't have to be cool. You can just be—"

He tripped over a leaf or an ant or something just as dangerous and

"AUGH!" *K-thud*

fell down the step.

But not just one step. That's not I.Q.'s style. Instead, he fell down every

"AUGH!" *K-thud*
"AUGH!" *K-thud*
"AUGH!" *K-thud*

step, until he landed face-first on the sidewalk.

"I.Q!" I shouted as I ran to him. "I.Q., are you all right?"

He looked up at me, kind of dazed.

"Listen," I said, "I have a better game than kickball."

"Yeah?" he asked hopefully.

"Yeah, it's called . . . 'Let's go to the computer store and check out the latest computers.'"

"Yeah?!" (He was getting a little excited.)

"Yeah, and after that, maybe we can swing by the library."

"Yeah!?" (He was getting *a lot* excited.)

"Yeah, and maybe then we can sharpen some pencils and—"

beep-beep-beep-beep

I stopped.

Splat glanced at me and gave an uneasy whine.

"Bernie . . . ," I.Q. asked.

"Yeah?"

beep-beep-beep-beep

"Is that your . . ." He swallowed. "Is that your underwear ringing?"

Splat whined louder.

beep-beep-beep-beep

"Uh . . . yeah." I coughed nervously.

beep-beep-beep-beep

"Well, maybe you should, like, you know, answer it."

I slowly nodded. But even as I dropped my head to begin talking to my underpants, I was thinking, *Oh no, here we go . . .*

beep-beep-beep-beep

again.